A GUIDE TO RESISTING PEER PRESSURE

A GUIDE TO MAKING YOUR OWN CHOICES

APOORV SHARMA

Made with ♥ on the Notion Press Platform
www.notionpress.com

FOR MY PARENTS, WHO GAVE ME EVERYTHING AND ALWAYS SEEM TO FIND A WAY TO GIVE MORE.

"Special thanks to my dear Mother,

Mrs.Neha Sharma

(My Inspiration and Strength)"

Contents

Acknowledgements   *ix*

1. What Is Peer Pressure ?   1

2. The Benefits Of Resisting Peer Pressure   4

3. Strategies For Resisting Peer Pressure   7

4. Coping With Peer Pressure In Specific Situations   10

5. Story 1   14

6. Story 2   17

Conclusion   21

From The Author   23

A Guide To Resisting Peer Pressure

Acknowledgements

First and foremost, I would like to thank all of the individuals who shared their personal experiences and insights with me while writing this book. Your willingness to open up and share your stories was invaluable, and I am grateful for your honesty and courage.

I would also like to thank my friends and family for their unwavering support and encouragement throughout the writing process. Your love and encouragement kept me going even when the going got tough.

Finally, I want to thank my readers. It is my hope that this book will provide valuable insights and guidance to those seeking to improve their lives and overcome the challenges they face. I am deeply grateful for the opportunity to share my ideas with you, and I hope that this book will inspire and empower you to make positive changes in your life.

Thank you.

Introduction:

Peer pressure is a natural part of growing up. It's the influence that friends, classmates, and other people our age have on us. While peer pressure can sometimes be positive, it can also be negative, leading us to make decisions that go against our own values and beliefs. This book is designed to help you understand and resist peer pressure so you can make your own decisions and be true to yourself.

Chapter 1: What is Peer Pressure?

In this chapter, we'll explore what peer pressure is and how it can impact us. We'll also discuss the different forms that peer pressure can take, including direct pressure, indirect pressure, and normative pressure.

Chapter 2: The Benefits of Resisting Peer Pressure.

In this chapter, we'll look at the benefits of resisting peer pressure. We'll discuss how making your own choices can help you develop self-confidence, independence, and critical thinking skills. We'll also talk about the consequences of giving in to peer pressure and how it can impact your personal growth and well-being.

Chapter 3: Strategies for Resisting Peer Pressure.

In this chapter, we'll provide practical strategies for resisting peer pressure. We'll talk about ways to stand up for yourself, such as using "I" statements and setting boundaries. We'll also discuss the importance of finding supportive friends and building a strong support system.

Chapter 4: Coping with Peer Pressure in Specific Situations.

In this chapter, we'll look at some common situations where peer pressure may be particularly strong, such as when it comes to alcohol, drugs, sex, and social media. We'll discuss ways to cope with peer pressure in these situations and how to make informed decisions that are right for you.

"It's better to walk alone than with a crowd going in the wrong direction. Do what you feel is right.. "

-Anonymous

CHAPTER ONE

What is Peer Pressure ?

Peer pressure is the influence that friends, classmates, and other people of our age have on us. It can be positive, leading us to try new things and challenge ourselves, or it can be negative, leading us to make choices that go against our own values and beliefs.

This topic is worth discussing but many of us have not ever tried to understand this and have been victims of peer pressure atleast once in our lives and have regretted later.So here in this book we will be discussing various aspects of peer pressure and how to deal with it .

> "*I would like to add that "**Peer Pressure is not an external pressure , it is the pressure you put on yourself to fit in.**" as no one can influence you without your permission and you must be driving your life towards your goals , instead of getting away with the thoughts of your friends.*"

There are three main forms of peer pressure:

1. Direct pressure : This is when someone directly asks or urges you to do something. For example, a friend might say, "Come on, just try it. Everyone else is doing it."

2. Indirect pressure : This is when someone tries to influence you through subtle hints or nonverbal cues. For example, a group of friends might give you a hard time if you don't want to go to a party or participate in a risky activity.

3 .Normative pressure : This is when we feel pressure to conform to the norms or expectations of a particular group. For example, we might feel pressure to dress a certain way or act a certain way in order to fit in with our friends or a particular social group.

Peer pressure can have both positive and negative impacts on us. On the positive side, it can help us try new things and challenge ourselves. It can also help us develop a sense of belonging and connection with others.

However, peer pressure can also have negative consequences. It can lead us to make choices that go against our own values and beliefs, or to engage in risky or harmful behaviors. For example, we might feel pressure to use drugs or alcohol even if we don't want to, or to engage in sexual activity before we're ready.

It's important to be aware of peer pressure and to have the skills to resist it when it goes against our own values and beliefs. This can help us make our own choices and be true to ourselves.

Examples:

• Samir is at a party with his friends and someone offers him a cigarette. He's never smoked before and doesn't really want to, but he's worried about what his friends will think if he says no. This is an example of direct pressure.

• Madhavi's friends are all posting pictures of themselves drinking and partying on social media. She doesn't really like to do all that , but she's worried that she'll be left out if she doesn't participate. This is an example of indirect pressure.

• Rishabh is a member of a sports team and the other members of the team are all wearing the same brand of clothes. He doesn't really like that brand or may be he thinks that those clothes are not worth the money spent, but he feels pressure to conform to the group norm and wear the same clothes. This is an example of normative pressure.

#Remember, it's important to be true to yourself and make your own choices, even if they're different from what your friends or peers are doing. It's okay to be different and it's important to take care of yourself and your own well-being.

:) (:

CHAPTER TWO

The Benefits of Resisting Peer Pressure

Now, we'll discuss the benefits of resisting peer pressure and making your own choices. Some of the benefits of resisting peer pressure include:

1. Building critical thinking skills: When you resist peer pressure, you're forced to consider your own values, beliefs, and goals. This can help you develop critical thinking skills, such as the ability to analyze situations and make informed decisions.

2. Avoiding negative consequences: Giving in to peer pressure can sometimes lead to negative consequences, such as getting into trouble with the law, damaging relationships, or putting yourself in danger. By resisting peer pressure, you can avoid these negative outcomes and protect your own well-being.

3. Maintaining authenticity: Resisting peer pressure can help you stay true to yourself and your own values and beliefs. This can be especially important during adolescence, when you're still figuring out who you are and what you stand for.

4. Building healthy relationships: By standing up for yourself and making your own choices, you can show others that you respect yourself and your own boundaries. This can help you build healthier and more fulfilling relationships with friends and others.

Overall, resisting peer pressure can have numerous benefits for your personal growth and well-being. It's important to be aware of the influence that others can have on us and to make decisions that are true to ourselves.

We need to be strong and confident enough to say NO to things which may harm us our family or anyone else in any way. Sometimes hanging out with friends is fun , but avoid such friends who ask you to bunk your classes or try involving you in any kind of illegal act . They may ask you for smoking and drinking alcoholic drinks , which they think us a status symbol or often teenagers find these habits to be COOL or to get a GANGSTA vibe . It's stupid dude , is this what your parents would appreciate once they get to know about.

Every time you think it's your life and you should experiment with this or you wanna try new things, just think about its consequences in long term.

A motivational speaker once said, "You are the average of the five people you spend the most time with." This means our close circle of peers can be seen as parts of ourselves. That is why we often find it difficult, even now, to go against the opinion of our family or friends because they are the people we care for most and do not want to disappoint , but at the same time being a human with working brains ; we should think twice before :

- Accelerating the car to 100 Kmph for false praise

OR

- Drinking 15 Glasses of water in 20 minutes for the sake of competition

OR

- Spending our parent's hard earned money mindlessly on expensive and useless article just to match the standards of our friends

OR

- Breaking our own personal rules and feeling guilty later Etc. All such situations can't be written ,but we ourselves know what all things we have ever done because of external influence or because of not being able to express our true opinion and what were the consequences of that act.

:)(:

CHAPTER THREE

Strategies for Resisting Peer Pressure

Peer pressure can be difficult to deal with, especially when you're young and still trying to figure out who you are and what you believe in. But it's important to remember that you have the power to resist peer pressure and make your own decisions. In this chapter, we present a number of strategies that can help you stand up for yourself and resist peer pressure.

1. Know Your Values and Beliefs: One of the best ways to resist peer pressure is to be clear about what you believe in and what's important to you.Take some time to reflect on what is important to you and what you stand for. This gives you a solid foundation to stand on when faced with peer pressure.

2. Use first-person sentences: When someone is trying to push you into something you don't want to do, it can be helpful to use first-person sentences to communicate your feelings and boundaries. For example, you could say something like "I appreciate your suggestion, but I'm not comfortable with it."I value my safety and well-being, and I need to make decisions that reflect my

values."

3. Have a plan: When you know you will find yourself in a situation where Pressure is on It can probably be helpful to have a plan. Think about what you will say or do if someone tries to pressure you, and have a back-up plan in case things don't go as expected.'

4. Find supportive friends: Surrounding yourself with supportive friends can be a great way to resist peer pressure. Find friends who share your values and beliefs and who respect your boundaries. These friends will be more likely to support you and help you resist peer pressure. # Avoid being with the people you think have bad character. As being friends with the guys who often use abusive language or always lies or show off a lot or disrespect the elders in any way or pass comments on other people. As they will always try to make these bad habits common for you and once you get trapped and start practicing these activities you may spoil you life.

5. Get support from others: If you're having trouble resisting peer pressure on your own, it can be helpful to get support from trusted adults, such as a parent, teacher, or counselor.These individuals can offer guidance, encouragement and a listening ear.

6. Practice saying no: Saying no to peer pressure can be difficult, especially if you're not used to it. But the more you practice, the easier it gets. Try acting out different scenarios with a trusted adult or friend, or practice saying no in your head or out loud.

7. Remember that it's okay to be different: Sometimes peer pressure can stem from a desire to fit in or be like others. But it's important to remember that it's okay to be different. In fact, staying true to yourself is often more rewarding and fulfilling than trying to be someone

you're not.In general, there are many strategies that can help you resist peer pressure.

8. Give excuses : For some people it may not be easy to say no , but it is important to learn this through practice but till then make excuses to avoid bad habits and use excuses to escape from such situations which arouse due to peer pressure.

For example :

if your friends ask you to roam around (time pass on streets) or anything else, just say that " Mumma has given me some urgent work to do" or "I am not feeling so well" or "Dad won't allow" or Anything else. I know making excuses is a superpower of most of us. So this time use it for s good cause.

The 8th strategy is the least recommended one , as you need to be strong enough to directly say no but if there is some case , use this. The most important thing is to find out what works best for you and stay true to yourself. Remember, you have the power to make your own decisions and stand up for what you believe in.

Although , this will always be advisable that you should be open and free enough to atleast any one person at your home to talk about your whole day at school and anything that happens to you , in any way be it academic, be it your friends talks or your attraction towards any other person.

:) (:

Coping with Peer Pressure in Specific Situations

In this chapter, we'll look at some common situations where peer pressure may be particularly strong, such as when it comes to alcohol, drugs, showing off, social media etc. We'll discuss ways to cope with peer pressure in these situations and how to make informed decisions that are right for you.

Some common situations where we often get trapped due to peer pressure and their solutions are given below :

1. Alcohol and drugs:

It's common for teens to feel pressure to try alcohol or drugs, especially if their friends are doing it. It's important to remember that you have the right to say "no" and to make your own decisions about your body. If you're not comfortable with the idea of drinking or using drugs, it's okay to say so. You can also consider alternative activities, such as going to a movie or having a game night.

2. Cheating on a test or assignment :

You may feel pressure from classmates to cheat on a test or assignment in order to get a good grade. It's important to remember that cheating is wrong and that it can have serious consequences, such as getting in trouble with your school or damaging your academic integrity. Instead of giving in to the pressure, consider seeking help from a teacher or tutor if you're struggling with the material.

#Remember , tests are conducted for the analysis of your academic progress , so that you would be aware of your position but while you cheat in tests you are cheating yourself. Deceiving to ourselves leads us to many problems later as we will never know what are actual capabilities are and it will keep us in dark or false pride of being a good student .

3. Conform to certain standards or expectations:

You may feel pressure from friends or classmates to conform to certain standards or expectations, such as wearing certain clothes or participating in certain activities. It's important to remember that you have the right to be yourself and to make your own choices, even if they differ from what others expect of you.

4. Engage in risky behaviors:

You may feel pressure from friends to engage in risky behaviors, such as driving too fast or engaging in dangerous sports. It's important to remember that you have the right to say "no" and to prioritize your own safety.

5. Skip class or cut school :

You may feel pressure from friends to skip class or cut school, especially if you're feeling bored or unengaged in your classes. It's important to remember that education is important and that skipping class or cutting school can have negative consequences, such as falling behind in your studies or getting in trouble with your school.

6. Relationships :

It is natural for teens to be curious about sex and relationships, but it's important to remember that you have the right to make your own decisions about when and with whom you have a relationship. If you feel pressured or influenced to get into a relationship before you're ready , just because every other friend of yours is into it ; it's okay to say "no". You can also consider alternative activities, such as talking to a trusted adult or friend about your feelings.

Until you don't have full faith on yourself and don't consider yourself to be a truly mature person avoid being indulged in relationships and all. This may also affect your mantal health. Teenage is an amazing phase to create friends and hangout with them. You may find it fun to create memories with friends but on the other hand it is important to balance the other things , which your parents and teachers expect from you.

7. Social media :

Social media can be a great way to stay connected with friends, but it can also be a source of pressure. You may feel pressure to post certain pictures or to act a certain way online. It's important to remember that you have control over what you post and how you present yourself online. If you're not comfortable with something, it's okay to say "no".

:)(:

CHAPTER FIVE

STORY 1

"Rishi Learns to Stand Up for Himself"

There was once a young boy named Rishi who lived in a small town with his parents and his sister. Rishi was a kind and friendly boy, but he sometimes struggled with standing up for himself and making his own decisions

One day, Rishi started a new school and met a group of boys who seemed really cool at first. They were popular and confident, and Rishi was excited to be friends with them.

However, as the days went by, Rishi started to notice that these boys were always trying to get him to do things he wasn't comfortable with. They would ask him to skip class or to lie to his parents about where he was going. They would also pressure him to try things he didn't want to try, like smoking or stealing.

At first, Rishi tried to resist the pressure, but it was hard. He didn't want to lose his new friends and he didn't want to be left out. So, he started to give in to their requests, even though deep down he knew it wasn't right.

As time went on, Rishi started to feel more and more guilty about his actions. He knew that he was doing things that went against his own values and beliefs, and he felt like he was letting himself down. He also started to worry about the consequences of his actions - what if he got in trouble with his parents or with the school? What if he got caught doing something he shouldn't be doing?

As time went on, Rishi started to feel more and more guilty about his actions. He knew that he was doing things that went against his own values and beliefs, and he felt like he was letting himself down. He also started to worry about the consequences of his actions - what if he got in trouble with his parents or with the school? What if he got caught doing something he shouldn't be doing?

"Rishi, you have to stand up for yourself, " she said firmly. "You can't let these boys pressure you into doing things that go against your values and beliefs. You are a good person and you deserve to be true to yourself."

Rishi's sister could see the tears welling up in his eyes as he listened to her words. She reached out and took his hand, giving it a reassuring squeeze.

"I know it's hard, Rishi, " she said softly. "But you have to be strong. You have the right to make your own decisions and to be true to yourself. And if you ever need help or support, you can always talk to me or Mom and Dad. We're here for you."

Rishi was grateful for his sister's advice and he knew that she was right. He made up his mind to stand up for himself and to be true to himself, no matter what. The next time his friends asked him todo something he didn't want to do, he stood up for himself and said no.

At first, his friends were surprised and disappointed, but they eventually respected his decision and stopped pressuring him.

Through this experience, Rishi learnt the importance of standing up for himself and making his own decisions. He also learnt the value of honesty and communication, and how they can help to strengthen relationships.

CHAPTER SIX

STORY 2

"Anu's Journey of Self-Discovery"

Anu had always been a good student and a responsible teenager. She was focused on her studies and her future, and she didn't have much interest in relationships. But everything changed when she started hanging out with a new group of friends.

Anu's new friends were all involved in relationships, and they would constantly talk about their partners and show off the gifts they received. Anu couldn't help but feel a little envious and left out. She also couldn't help but notice that her friends seemed happier and more popular than ever before. She started to feel like something was missing in her own life and that she was missing out on all the fun.

One day, one of Anu's friends introduced her to a cute guy from another school. He was charming, generous, and he seemed to really like Anu. Before she knew it, Anu was swept up in a whirlwind romance. She was constantly texting and talking to her new boyfriend, and she was thrilled when he started showering her with gifts and attention.

Anu's parents were a little worried about her sudden change in behavior, but they trusted her and hoped that she was making good decisions. They didn't realize that Anu was starting to feel a lot of pressure from her boyfriend to do things she wasn't comfortable with. He was always asking her to skip class and lie to her parents, and he would get angry and upset if she didn't do what he wanted.

As time went on, Anu's grades started to suffer and she started to feel overwhelmed and stressed. She knew that she was sacrificing her studies and her future for the sake of her relationship, and she was starting to regret getting involved. She also knew that she was risking getting caught and getting in trouble with her parents and the school.

One day, Anu had had enough. She was tired of feeling like she had to constantly please her boyfriend and her friends, and she was sick of sacrificing her own goals and values. She knew that she needed to stand up for herself and resist the pressure from her boyfriend. So, she gathered up her courage and had a difficult conversation with him.

At first, Anu's boyfriend was surprised and upset. He didn't understand why she was suddenly changing her tune and he worried that he would lose her as a girlfriend. He tried to sweet talk her and convince her to stay with him, but Anu was firm in her decision. She explained that she didn't want to do things that went against her values and beliefs, and that she needed to focus on her studies and her future.

The conversation with her boyfriend was tough, but it was worth it. Anu felt a weight lifted off her shoulders as she stood up for herself and asserted her own needs and desires. She knew that it wasn't going to be easy to break free from the cycle of peer pressure and toxic relationships, but she was determined to do what was best for herself.

As she worked on rebuilding her relationships with her parents and her friends, Anu also started to work on rebuilding her confidence and her sense of self. She learned the importance of standing up for herself and making her own decisions, and she was grateful for the support and understanding of those who were around her in times of need.

Conclusion

In this book, we've explored what peer pressure is and how it can impact us. We've also discussed the benefits of resisting peer pressure and provided practical strategies for doing so. Remember, making your own choices and being true to yourself is important for your personal growth and well-being. Don't be afraid to stand up for yourself and resist peer pressure when it goes against your values and beliefs.

• *The traits that put you at higher risk for falling in to the peer pressure trap include:*

° Low self esteem.
  ° Lack of self confidence.
  ° Uncertainty about ones place within a given peer group.
  ° No personal interests exclusive of one's peer group.
  ° Fear of rejection from a social group.
  ° Feeling isolated from peers and/or family.
  ° Poor academic abilities or performance.
  ° Personal confusion and anxiety.
  ° Being excessively shy or nervous.

• *Some effective ways to beat peer pressure are:*

° Simply say "No".
  ° Openly say that it's a bad idea.
  ° Build Confidence
  ° Make a long term goal.
  ° Make a joke of the situation.

° Give an excuse why you can't.

° Suggest a different activity.

° Leave the situation.

Peer pressure is not always bad , sometimes it also proves to be helpful for us when we take it positively and have ourselves in a good , intelligent and hard working peer group that motivates us to put extra efforts for our goals. But that only happens when we have good understanding about ourselves and people around us.

I hope these will help you be confident and take wise decisions especially during teenage as this the time we easily get manipulated and face many problems due to a sense of insecurity and confusions that arise in our day to day lives

From The Author

Dear reader,

I hope you have enjoyed reading this book on peer pressure and that you have found it helpful and informative.

Peer pressure is a common and often difficult challenge that you , me and many of us face at some point in our lives. It can be especially challenging for young people, who may be navigating new social situations and trying to figure out who they are and what they believe in.

By gifting this book to your friends or young siblings, you can help them to better understand the dynamics of peer pressure and how to cope with it. You can also show them that you care about their well-being and that you want to support them as they navigate these challenging but important years.

So, if you found this book helpful and you know someone who could benefit from reading this book, I encourage you to consider gifting it to them. You never know - it could make a big difference in their lives.

Thank you for your support, and I hope you continue to find this book helpful and informative.

With Love,

Apoorv Sharma